Soaring

Soaring

An Odyssey
of the Soul

Roger Elwood

BAKER BOOK HOUSE
Grand Rapids, Michigan 49516

. . . that when the flood

is past, I may Thy eternal

brightness see and share

Thy joy at last.

—Inscription on
the tombstone of
Fletcher Christian

11:53 A.M.

My name is William.

I just died.

My eyes open . . .

Scared?

No one can really know how he will feel when The Moment comes. I always bragged to those who would listen that death held no terrors whatever for me, that God would be there the instant It happened—and He would welcome me with open arms and—.

He isn't.

I'm alone.

Utterly.

I can sense that. I am nowhere and yet I know I have to be somewhere. Only atheists believe that the grave is the end—and the body turns to dust and that's that. But I am not one of those. I believe. I accept.

I . . .

Scared?

I am.

God, help — —!

Tick — -tick — — — —

A clock?

Not here!

I'm imagining it.

Yes, that's it. You can't scuttle the habits, the patterns of a lifetime in a few minutes. Nowhere in the Bible does there appear the suggestion that *everything* is erased. Sin, yes; human failings, yes; all those little hangups that plague us—that's all past tense now; I must remember this—I must say: that *plagued* us. But some things must surely remain or we would be like amnesiacs, and amnesia is a disease, and we are to be free of such.

I'm rambling a bit. But I can't *see* anything. I . . .

Myself . . .

I am looking at myself.

Not in a mirror.

Not a reflection.

I am looking at my body.

The eyes are closed. The chest does not move. The face is pale.

Am I losing my mind? Absurd! Insanity in Heaven? No, just dislocation. Getting used to —

—and the thought strikes me, hard, like a bomb exploding inches away —

—being *outside* my body. How incredible! The thought of . . .

Death . . .

Hard to think of it as death, this state in which I find myself. There is no cessation of consciousness. Even the turmoil is passing. (You can tell, can't you?) I am making more sense now. There is not so much a kaleidoscopic aura to everything. People used to say that a dying man saw the important moments of his life flashing before his mind's eye in an instant. But I know now that a dead man glimpses the moments after death much more vividly. At the outset it is a little like *watching* a melodrama on some movie screen, without actually ever being involved—though indeed I am a pivotal character.

Woman:
William? Dear God, William!

Minister:
He's gone . . .

Woman:
N-o!

Minister:
Yes, he's . . .

A Scream — Tears

The woman falls, sobbing, against the frail, unmoving body on the bed. Her son tries to restrain her but he cannot. He waits as the minister bends over her and whispers into her ear. Apparently the right words have been said—and have had their effect, however temporary. She still cries but pulls back and sinks into a nearby chair. She has lost someone very important to her, someone without whom she has always thought she could not go on living. For many weeks, in fact, she will *not* want to live but, afterward, with her two children by her side, somehow she . . .

And so it goes, this observing everything without being a participant. Like looking at my loved ones through a one-way glass and . . .

My eyes seem to close or at least vision fades. It is as though a momentary lull comes so that I may be calmed. But before this period of cessation, I receive a momentary glimpse of the Savior, the blessed Christ, He is smiling at me, and I feel calmed by His radiance.

Then . . .

Weeping.

The sound comes to me cloaked in night. Sarah, my wife, is in bed, weeping.

If only I could be with her. If only . . .

I am!

By an act of will I am in the room with her, with my beloved. I shout a hello, my hand reaches out to touch her, as I had done so often during the years of the flesh (I call them that so easily after so short a period of being anything but flesh), yet she doesn't budge even slightly. She acts as though she never heard me. Or felt me.

I am bending over her, watching tears fall from her eyes and form little spots of wet cloth on the pillow beneath her head.

The remarkable bond Sarah and I had enabled us to survive even the tragedies of life. And life, after all, is basically tragedy, is it not? There are moments of joy, there are periods of exaltation, but the rest is pain of one sort or another. God gives us the happiness to get us through the anguish. Scripture speaks of this vale of tears that is life. As usual, God's Word is never less than right on the mark.

Our first child lived only a few days after birth. (What had become of *his* soul? Was he just to be lost, a speck blown away by the winds of eternity, unimportant because he existed for only a brief fraction of time? Perhaps I will soon find out. Perhaps he will be presented to me as he was then, tiny, yet different: and he'll be healthy, his skin pink and clean and . . . Or, perhaps, it will be that he comes up to me, eternally mature, and handsome, and says, "Father, I am John," his strong face radiant. And I will hold him in my arms and weep tears of joy.)

That tragedy was exceedingly hard to endure. Years later we could look back and see that it made my dearest and I closer than before it happened, but what awful melancholy we suffered at the time. We found ourselves questioning God, asking Him in agonized prayer: Why, why, why, why . . . Over and over. . . . We would visit John's grave, stand

18

there by the headstone and let the tears roll down our cheeks. I would put my arms around my beloved, and she would lean on me, sobbing.

And then, somehow, we just accepted. We came to understand that, whatever we did, the baby would still be dead, his body cold and limp, his skin a strange blue shade. What good would it do to weep and scream and beat ourselves emotionally bloody over a fact that was *unchangeable?*

To share life was marvelous; to share a loved one's death was awful. Yet the sharing carried the seeds of mutual need and strength which, in our case, were allowed to blossom and grow. With other people how often do these seeds remain dormant, and the tragedies that could have cemented relationships render them meaningless instead, ripping the mourners asunder?

Even after the process of adjustment had begun, the house nevertheless seemed emptier, as though John had actually lived there with us. For a while we went into the room that had been furnished for him, and stood there in its midst and felt crushed again by our sorrow. For a while. . . .

We did many such things—the graveside pilgrimage, the rest of it all as the children of mourning. And then this period ended. It ended as Sarah and I walked among the oaks and pines on our land and took in deep breaths of air laced with the scents of country life. We looked up at the sky, clear, scarcely a cloud to blemish it, and we knew that the time had come to pray for another child. No emotional scene, no sudden burst of spiritual revelation, just a quiet walk. We buried our sorrow in the scattered leaves of fall.

Dear Sarah, my love . . .

There were other sorrows, of course, moments involving the loss of our own parents. I remember my father who died with some words on his lips that I could never forget, for he said, "I see the child, I see the child." I knew what he meant, and that simple claim reinforced our belief that we would see our beloved son again. Dad loved him every bit as much as Sarah and I did, and he went into a period of mourning nearly as deep as our own. Mom, too, but she had a habit of maintaining a surface cheerfulness, whatever the circumstances. I sometimes found this irritating because it seemed artificial, and often ill-conceived, but it was deep-down sincere, a gift Mom had, and one we all found to be the greatest possible blessing during the months after our son died, and, also, after Dad's death.

I snap back to the present but nothing has changed. She cries on, her sobs reaching me and making me want to embrace her but, for Sarah, suddenly I don't exist. I will never hold her again in the way that I had done for more than half a century.

My wife, without whom I thought I couldn't live, is a widow . . .

I discover something about myself. I have a body, yes; I can see the fingers, the toes, the arms, everything about me. Yet sight is not in the conventional way, but through special "eyes," as though I am wearing glasses of a unique sort. And I am fully clothed but in a strange, radiant sort of material, so radiant that it seems made of—yes—made of sunlight. If only I had a mirror, I could see my face. But then I might not be able to recognize my own countenance.

I reach up to touch my cheek.

Smooth.

The skin is smooth. The wrinkles are gone. The scars don't exist. And my hair . . . soft, flowing. I am spirit yet I am substance, in a strange and quite wonderful way.

Rebirth!

That word pauses on my lips, then is spoken in a hush. I have truly been born again, in an even more significant way than when I accepted Christ as Savior and Lord of my life. Realizing what it signifies, I jump up, half-expecting the pain of arthritis, half-expecting to collapse in a rickety heap of enfeebled flesh and bones and thin blood pumping through an aging heart that will soon skip a beat, then another, and eventually not beat at all.

But, no, youth has returned and yet something beyond youth. Unexplainable just now.

After leaving Sarah's room, I walk for miles without being tired. The time is autumn. Leaves flutter and skip all around me, yes *through* me as well. (At first this fosters an uncomfortable feeling, but something within me — or is it really without — quiets the uneasiness, like whispered words of calm.)

Obviously I *am* present here in this assemblage of oak trees, and tall scaly barked pine, and I can *see* a great deal: birds flying overhead; a hop-toad jumping across a slate pathway; a squirrel scampering down a trunk — it pauses, cocking its head, listening, and then disappears back up the same trunk. (Has it sensed me? Animals may have senses beyond those possessed by human beings, I had always privately conjectured. Perhaps dogs howl after their masters have died because they sense a lingering presence, but one they can't *see*, and that howl is born of frustration.)

Yet being present and being a *part* of the scene are not the same, else why would leaves pass right through me or the ground reveal no prints after my passage?

I come on a road—a familiar thoroughfare. In life I drove along it many times, but in life I could reach out and grip the steering wheel of my car and honk the horn and stop for red lights and. . . . I was part of the world around me, and it was part of me, through the intake of sight and sound and smell and touch, all merging within my brain in that wonderful interaction of the body's systems that man-made creations could never duplicate.

On the corner ahead, looking slightly rundown, is a country store. I stopped there many times, bought milk, pastries, any of the other items that Sarah needed but occasionally neglected to get when we journeyed much farther to a large supermarket in another community. I could go in and listen to Ed Petersen spouting off and—no, I decide that that is not what I wish. (During my life—I know I *am* alive now but, somehow, the thought patterns of a generation seem reluctant to loosen their grip on my consciousness—anyway, *back then,* I would from time to time wonder what people really thought of me, perhaps even allowing this to obsess me at such moments. But it matters not the slightest bit anymore, this human pettiness.) Instead I turn across the road, to a large pond beside it, and stand there by the edge, half-expecting to see myself in the water. When I don't, momentary panic nibbles at me but then calm and peace reassume control.

And then something odd happens. (Isn't all that transpires from now on "odd" if one defines that word as an event or series of events out of the commonplace, unexperienced, unknown until they play themselves out before your eyes?)

I am watching a bird soaring through the sky. I think it is a meadowlark, its flight graceful, first in an arch, then a straight line, zooming toward the earth and then up again, spinning and rising and swooping and soaring.

As a child I envied these creatures of the air. Man could soar only by clumsy imitation in a monstrously heavy invention of metal, plastic, rubber, and glass, at enormous expense; a thing soaking up fuel and requiring maintenance crews and, indeed, a great deal else. But a bird, born from a single fragile egg, in just a short while could take off on its own. Its life has not been spotted by

An Odyssey of the Soul

countless hundreds of millions of human beings, and truly it has been born hidden, isolated, in a tree, alone except for the faithful mother and those others of its own kind that will survive the same nest. And it would die the same way, unnoticed by the outside world. One day too old to soar any longer, too old even to leave the ground; oh, it would flip and squirm and try ever so hard but it would fail, and then would fall over and die.

But—the thought is born—what if I could now soar as the birds or the angels just by willing this to happen.

I hesitate.

And then, instantly, as instantly as the thought had been born, I leave the ground.

Soaring!

Can it be so? Or is it delusion?

No, it is real. I am, I truly am . . . soaring.

To be in the midst of such an incredible feat and yet be not even momentarily afraid is a surprise transcending that of the feat itself. I am flying— alone, mechanically unaided, propelling myself simply by the desire of my mind to do so.

For an instant—and it can be only that since my mental "wings" hesitate just for the briefest passage of time, (another image from that other life I know, for the state in which I find myself now is not hampered by time, which really doesn't exist anyway, except in the mechanical constructions devised by man in the form of clocks and sundials and instruments containing dripping sand)—for that instant (or whatever), think of the significance of three words: journey to Heaven.

When would it be? When would this beguiling prelude end, this warming up of the orchestra before the symphony itself?

And what would Heaven be like? Marching according to a celestial tune? In line? Single file? An eternity ahead of me . . . but what else? Will Moses be there to greet me? Elijah?

The thought passes, at least in that form. Heaven was being viewed through the telescope of earth's finiteness. Man filtering through the still clinging mortality of flesh-and-blood recollections what would be utterly, entirely divine.

I continue my soaring, brushing absurdities out of my mind. The reality would come soon enough.

Below me is New York City.

How it all comes back to me, not great moments of epochal impact on our lives but pleasant little memories like . . . yes, that first time and only time my beloved and I stopped together at the Teheran, a wonderful Middle Eastern restaurant on 44th Street, down the block from the famous old Algonquin Hotel. A couple of years passed before we made it back, and then, sadly, we discovered that the restaurant had been torn down, a victim of the prejudices generated in the wake of the Iranian hostage crisis in the latter part of the 1970s.

We found another place at which we could eat, and although the food was truly among the very best we had eaten anywhere, it was not as memorable as the Teheran, appreciated as much for the head waiter as the food.

I had gone alone on business for quite some time, stopping at that restaurant at the end of the day, enjoying it each time. But then there was a break that lasted several years, and I found myself honestly missing the Teheran. I knew my beloved would enjoy it, so I asked her to take time off from the children and the housework. After getting an elderly woman from church to take care of them, we drove into New York City, and while I took care of a few quick appointments, Sarah did some shopping, and then we headed for the Teheran.

The restaurant section happened to be on the second floor of a quite narrow building, and we had had to wade through the smoke-filled bar area. Both of us were amazed at how lemming-like people could be, with their cigarettes and cigars — the smoke was so thick that it seemed similar to what the London fog must have been like a quarter of a century earlier — and their liver-corroding, brain-destroying alcohol. Finally we reached the top of a long floor of steps.

The same head waiter greeted us. After taking our coats, he turned to me, and asked, "Will you have your usual chicken soraya, sir? Would the Mrs. like to try it?"

I was flabbergasted, and showed it. How could he have remembered me after so long?

The man simply smiled good-naturedly at the expression on my face, and took Sarah and me to the same table that I had sat at during the earlier dinners in that restaurant!

How many people touched my life once in sweet little moments like that? None can be said to have changed the course of history. But they were part of being human . . . the good part.

I think of stopping at the Empire State Building, strolling in Central Park. And immediately I retract that thought—everything is different now and my newfound ability is far too important to be wasted on earthly pursuits. (Yet was Heaven to turn me from the light, pleasant little moments—harmless caprices, as it were—that occasionally prevailed in mortal life?)

I am growing aware of yet another aspect of my new form, this state into which death has plunged me and which has been for me like the metamorphosis from inside some cosmic cocoon: Down There I was a worm, groveling in the dust, but Up Here I am a butterfly, soaring from flower to flower, sampling the nectar, enjoying the sweetness, and then on again to another, and another. Even this analogy breaks down, ultimately, for there is a marked contrast: flight for the butterfly ends with

finality, not in rebirth but instead a cessation of
wind through gossamer wings, a struggling against
unknown, impeding forces puzzling, undoubtedly.
For creatures have not the awareness of death that
human beings do; it is just an ending to them, a final
curtain of sorts, the nothingness of being trampled
on by rubber soles or framed with others of its kind
behind glass, to be hung on a wall or to be pulled
apart by cruel young fingers. But for the human
species, made in a divine image (and with astonish-
ing impact this ancient truth envelops my whole
spirit), yes, for me . . . flight is the beginning, an
odyssey with remarkable ramifications.

I soar on and on, with no sensation of being tired.
Could it have been for hours? Even days? (An
entrapment of chronology, true, but just as red is
red and green is green, some labels from Down
There will — I become more and more convinced —
remain whether or not they are pertinent or merely
residual images. They will be recalled as frames of
reference when the former life is thought of, fleet-
ingly. It would not be possible to discard everything; even God himself spoke to man in the terms
that man could understand. And if man is to be
welcomed into God's Heaven, that bridge of com-
munication would surely remain, at least until sup-
planted by orientations more wholly divine.)

I continue going from country to country. I see places I dreamed of seeing when I was my old self; when I would have had to take a plane or board an ocean liner; when the cost had been too much for me to afford earlier in that life and then, when I had had enough to spend, I was too old and tired and ill to stand the exertion, so I lapsed into conjuring up visions in fitful bouts of daydreaming . . . the Egyptian pyramids, the mountains of Switzerland, the lochs of Scotland, the ruins of Greece and Italy, all the spots that movies and television had impressed on me, had burned into me as desirable. But at last they are now before my eyes, in reality, not fantasy.

And I come down from the sky and land on the dome of the Taj Mahal to watch the sun sparkle off the huge pool in front and dance along the rows of always green trees on either side. (I have dislodged an exotic-looking bird which must have sensed me and, searching frantically for the intruder but finding no one, it goes squawking off into the sky, a blur of colors and noise.)

I sit there for quite a while, my eyes searching for miles in all directions. I have the world at my feet, and I am resting on the very top of one of the most legendary structures in all of man's history! (And, what seems at once an eternity, and yet mere seconds ago, I was dying, my breath coming ragged, my eyes rolling in their sockets. Then those eyes closed, the breathing ceased, body systems halting for all time — an end soon to be transformed into an altogether new beginning.)

From the Taj Mahal I go elsewhere. How wondrous it is — by mere thought — to be freed from physical limitations. Instantaneously, in the twinkling of an eye, I can soar from one spot on the globe to another, without the sensation of rapid travel as in a jet plane or a high-speed transit system.

As I do all this, I become aware of something else that is strange, at first completely inexplicable but, shortly after, sensed with growing understanding.

Anguish.

I do not feel it myself, for that would be a contradiction of God's promise about the spiritual state after death, but know that it is being endured by others. This understanding comes to me in much

Soaring

the same manner as knowledge of the torment of the rich man in Hell came to Lazarus.

I land once again. I am on the pathway leading to the Tower of London. I see the aged stones, the massiveness of the structure. It is a chilling sight, for it is a scene of death, its confines the last earthly residence of so many doomed human beings. I turn away, shivering slightly.

Suddenly, I am in another land, this time a desert place, with tanks rolling across the sand, explosions, screams, and bodies of young boys blown into uncountable pieces, their youth ground to red pulp.

And other areas of pain and suffering, ancient and modern, flash before me in rapid succession, the penalty of human sin laid out in a tapestry of anguish. I see most victims after their bodies have become limp and cold but I do glimpse a few in the actual process of dying and it is as though they likewise see me, for their eyes are filled with pleading, their lips moving in wordless supplication.

Everywhere I look it is the same: the ghettos of New York, the slums of London, the battlegrounds of Northern Ireland, the Middle East, South America, Africa, so many inhabited spots on the tortured globe that is Man's world . . . people behaving violently toward one another, letting hatred and

Soaring

jealousy and ambition tear them away from God's plan for their lives.

I feel suspiciously close to weeping but there are to be no more tears for me. What Mankind suffers is hardly a sentence imposed by an unfeeling Divinity, but rather a malady of the race's own concoction. Eons ago, before the Fall, it was different, but that time can never be recaptured, at least in the span of mortal existence.

As these thoughts continue, I feel myself yearning for some final contact with my family: Sarah and our children. To feel, in such a flood, the collective sins of the Human Race stretches even my new spiritual endurance; for in that rush of global torment, I begin to comprehend why there is a Heaven and a Hell, why some are doomed and others are rewarded. Man's basic nature would demand punishment or else justice would be a hollow thing, an exercise in self-mockery. What some view as the cruel acts of a hateful God are really the traps set not by Him but by those who have become neurotic, irrational creatures, blind and insensitive to that which is holy and divine, rummaging about in the slime of their transgressions or clinging as moronic bats to darkened cave walls, with the sunlight but a brief flight away.

Sarah . . .

Finally, I turn from these considerations, from three billion lives to just one, from the Taj Mahal back to a small house in the country, a house surrounded by tall oak and pine, with a little brook forming one boundary line.

Suddenly, I am there: Sarah and Ellen and Michael are leaving. Their heads are bowed in sorrow. They are on their way to my burial; if they only knew what it was like for me, perhaps the tears would dry quickly. . . .

I have felt regret over the sins of Mankind, it is true, but joy is returning now and sad images are being brushed away. If I had lived my life differently, my destiny would have been altogether

Soaring

changed. But, no, I accepted in faith the way He laid out before me, and that was cause for rejoicing.

Their tears, my jubilance, I think wistfully. They cry because I have left but that very departure has opened up a life of incredible fulfillment. Not even the inspired prose of Old and New Testaments could more than hint at the excitement that was beginning to infuse itself into my consciousness. This excitement was not altogether inside me, that is, coming *from* me but also excitement coming *to* me. (Could it be Heaven's call, the collective voices of millions of redeemed men, women and children, joined with a choir of angels, ready to usher in yet another soul saved from the harsh but necessary reality of damnation?)

Oh, Lord, I say in my thoughts and my feelings, *oh, blessed Lord*. . . .

I know that soon I will begin the most breathtaking segment of my incredible odyssey. . . .

Over the years men everywhere have in jest or utter seriousness voiced the desire to be at their own funerals, to see how people would react to their deaths, to learn how much of the affection expressed in life would remain after death's curtain fell.

I remember how hypocritical some of those at various funerals had been. The only reason people attended was for "appearances" and then with the greatest reluctance. As soon as they left the mortuary, they would start talking about the deceased, freed by his death from any inhibitions they might have otherwise felt. They would jump on the personality of the one who died, how very cheap he was, how mean, what a vicious temper he had, and whatever else they could unearth in their minds

Soaring

about him. And, ultimately the worst hypocrisy of all was revealed by relatives fighting over the deceased's last will and testament, scrambling for pieces of his estate like ravenous jackals moving in on a fresh corpse. . . .

Now, here I am, watching the people I associated with during my life, listening to what they whisper to one another.

"It's hard to believe."

"I know. Except for that one bit of illness, he was as healthy as could be."

"That's all it takes—one siege. The body, with age, simply isn't as combative in terms of disease."

"Sarah's taking it pretty well."

"For now, yes, but later, when she's really alone in that house, alone for the first time, she'll break down."

"A pattern, isn't it?"

"Always. I've had several members of my family die, and we reacted the same way each time."

"I used to think that the sandwiches and coffee and pastries after the funeral seemed grossly insensitive—too much of a celebration."

"No more?"

"No. I'm convinced it relieves the tension, offers a break in the pattern of tragedy. A fleeting break, I know, but better than none at all."

Heads nod. Tears well up, trickle over bottom lids and edge down cheeks.

Sarah . . .

In the front row, with Ellen and Michael.

Outwardly, none of them displays very much emotion. They are being quite proper, quite dignified.

I stand next to my wife, my widow, and try to rest my hand on her shoulder but realize, again, the uselessness of the gesture — and move away, toward the back of the chapel. More whispers drift past my ears.

"It always seems as though a presence lingers at funerals, don't you think?"

"Yes, indeed. As if the person is reluctant to leave even though he has no choice in the matter."

"But the Bible teaches that to be absent from the body is to be present with God. Doesn't that pre-suppose an instantaneous transition, dead one minute, with Him the next?"

A pause.

"But time doesn't really exist. We construct it mechanically but, apart from this, it's just not real. God uses such descriptions as time merely for our sakes, so that we can comprehend everything."

Soaring

The men having this discussion are standing in the rear of the chapel. I wish I could reveal to them how much of what they say is true. . . .

As the service begins, the excitement that commenced within me a short while before intensifies. I think back to my high school and college graduation ceremonies. Those were beginnings; in a similar way this funeral is equally portentous. For the people attending it, the service is a finale, a conclusion, the end of a life and a whole series of relationships; but for me it is to be the point of departure, a wondrous commencement.

The whispering ceases. Everyone turns to the front. Ellen and Michael stand up and face those gathered—dozens of mourners—and start singing my favorite hymn, Abide *With Me.* More tears flow.

And then my friend the minister gives his eulogy. He talks of God's unfathomable love for Man and His plan of salvation. At moments such as these, he says, it is comforting to know that loved ones have been redeemed by Christ's sacrifice at Calvary.

He speaks of the sadness the atheist and other ungodly ones must know, standing by the grave of a wife, a daughter, a mother, a father . . . for according to the atheist's views, *that* is the end. There'll never be another reunion.

I think of how terribly, terribly correct he is, this friend of mine in life, but then I am not now dead so I must stop separating that life from *this* life and calling the latter death. I am — as a matter of fact, a transcendent, glorious fact — more alive than I can ever remember previously being, with a clarity that defies the ability of language to express it, as ironic as that sounds.

This minister, this sincere man of faith (unlike others on the scene, the kind who ask for money time-and-time again, who barter prayer and healing and spiritual gifts for contributions), this dear friend points out the hope and joy that fill the heart of the believer in God through the ministry of the Holy Spirit. God transforms him from corruption to incorruption, mortality putting on immortality.

But here the service is interrupted — by a man I only distantly remember. He stands, impressively tall with neat gray hair, but trembling as he says apologetically, "Please forgive me for doing this, but I have to say something."

He pauses briefly, as if to gain strength for a great task. Eyes turn toward him. He seems to gain confidence, so he continues: "I've fought the Lord a long time. I've refused His every overture of love and mercy. Just a month ago my wife lay dying, and her last plea to me was: 'Let me go to my Savior knowing that you have accepted Him as your own Savior and Lord.'"

He breaks down, sobbing, but quickly regains control. "I was not able to tell that wonderful Christian woman what she wanted to hear. That's been torturing me ever since the day she died. But today I know what I must do. I'm going to give my life to the Lord, seeking His forgiveness for my sins and committing my life to Him in obedience to His will."

Then, as though realizing where he is, and looking at the minister, he says with contrition, "Please forgive the intrusion," smiles again at the audience as though he and God now have a secret, and returns to his seat.

Sensing that further lengthy comment will be anticlimactic, the minister makes a few appropriate remarks and closes with a beautiful prayer for Sarah and our children.

Respectful "Amens" from the listeners cause me suddenly to focus on their sorrow. It is a kind of tribute; if I were not missed they would not cry. And if mere platitudes had been voiced just now, there would be utter silence, not the murmurs of assent.

Finally, it all draws to a close. Ellen and Michael sing another hymn and then the time has come for the mourners to file past the casket. In the background an organ plays softly.

I join the line and walk past the body which my spirit once occupied. I pause and look—the skin chill, the face rigid, like a piece of marble sculpture. Under one hand is a pocket Bible I had used often, the pages dog-eared, the binding nearly gone. (I remember, when my father died, decades before, I slipped a small hunting knife he cherished into a pocket of his burial suit. It is true that the dead cannot use such items; an old, tattered Bible or a rusty knife are of no value to them, but such acts are necessary for the living, necessary as some final evidence of the love that still bound them to the deceased.) Finally, it is Sarah's turn; she places a kiss on the body's forehead, as Ellen and Michael bow their heads. Within minutes of this, the chapel is empty, save for the pallbearers.

Outside, there is talk of me again but not a word of criticism, not a single bit of profanity used. All the slightly neurotic imaginings of life—the "who is really my friend" syndrome—have been proved stupid and unfounded. I have no enemies. I conducted my life as God seemed to desire, and I know now that these mourners accepted me into their lives because they wanted to do so, because I was a desirable friend, someone they could trust and—

and . . . love. That word —*love*— stays in my mind.
All the many Bible verses dealing with it occur to
me in a flash but one group in particular stands out:

> *Though I speak with the tongues of men and of*
> *angels, and have not charity, I am become as sound-*
> *ing brass, or a tinkling cymbal.*

> *And though I have the gift of prophecy, and*
> *understand all mysteries, and all knowledge; and*
> *though I have all faith, so that I could remove*
> *mountains, and have not charity, I am nothing.*

> *And though I bestow all my goods to feed the poor,*
> *and though I give my body to be burned, and have*
> *not charity, it profiteth me nothing.*

I had known so many individuals who never learned to love, who perhaps were unable to open their hearts to others, who sealed themselves off from being involved, emotional hermits living in some secluded social forest, NO TRESPASSING signs hanging from their necks. That was never my way. It was never Sarah's. I desperately hope my death does not change her.

In a short while the service is resumed, at the burial plot. Most of those at the chapel have made the short trip. A few—elderly friends not up to facing the now chill autumn breezes—went home, wiping their eyes.

I am standing before my casket . . . in the midst of a farewell that men have faced (and feared) for thousands of years. Across from me are the three members of my immediate family. Some flowers are tossed on the casket after the minister has spoken one final time.

The mourners turn and walk away. Sarah goes halfway to the car, then returns to the grave, standing there, her head bowed. I see her lips moving but cannot hear what she says. Ellen and Michael guide her back to the car. She pauses, her head turning to the grave. She starts back toward it again, almost falls, but Michael holds her up and helps her to the grave. I reach out to her, telling her I am here, telling her that one day we will be together again, that this is only a temporary thing: *Please, my love, it is a* beginning. *You must believe that!*

But of course, for her there are no words; she can hear nothing of me, know nothing of my presence. The casket containing my body will soon be lowered into the ground, and she will try to get on with whatever life is left for her without me.

I want to go with her. I want to ride in the car back to our home and spend a few more minutes. But I do not. I stand here in the cemetery, watching attendants throwing dirt into my grave. Then the sod is placed on top. The marker will be along in a day or so. But for that short span of time you could walk by and never know that someone named William is buried there.

Another word escapes my lips, the last word I will ever utter on earth, earth corruptible and poisoned, earth of the beautiful forests and the toxic waste dumps, that place of pain and redemption.

Good-bye, I say. *Good-bye . . .*

Suddenly I am taken up.

That's the best way I can describe what is happening. It is not my ability to soar that is responsible this time. I haven't consciously willed myself to leave the ground. Instead I am *pulled* away, rapidly, and before I know it, I am looking down from an extremely high altitude, suspended. Oddly I am uninterested in moving, even slightly, for I know that everything is in Someone else's control, and Heaven cannot be far away now. The earthly leg of my odyssey is nearly concluded. (I realize with stunning finality that part of my existence will *never* be revisited—and yet I feel not at all sad. The door to my past is shut; there is no need to open it, even for an instant, because another door stretches out before me, wide open.)

As I remain motionless, it is as though my eyes see as never before, and, of course, that is quite the case: scales have fallen from me, the veil lifted as God has promised. I no longer see through a glass darkly. I. . . .

From all over the earth, I watch other spirits ascend to the same "plain" on which I am "stationed." (This "plain" couldn't be any more real than if it had been made of rock or concrete.)

The exodus is a continuous one, like that of the Jews from Egypt but without the tribulations of their wilderness years.

But many spirits are not joining us, my mind beams.

"That is right," I hear a voice answer.

I turn and see—yes!!!—*an angel.*

And even more incredibly, he has what could be wings though nothing like those pictured in man's great works of art.

"But how did you—?" I ask out loud.

"Have you not read that God judges the thoughts and intents of the heart?"

Of course—the angel read my mind!

And then he is gone. But I sense his presence, as though he will appear again, whenever perplexity threatens.

I watch those spirits going elsewhere. Their faces are not happy; instead anguish is written all over them. I. . . .

The angel again!

"Because their lives were filled with all manner of evil—because they chose not to repent and honor God."

"And they are being punished?"

"Yes."

"In Hell?"

"Yes."

Just as I had pondered earlier, just as I had witnessed the pain and suffering man had brought on himself through his lust, his greed, his erecting of images that he worshiped in place of God, I recognize, now, the justice of Hell, the need for it, the tragedy that it was there, which intensified my awareness that Hell couldn't be avoided as long as men ignored God, and molested little girls, and shotgunned whole families in their homes, and raped and tortured young boys, robbed, maimed, killed, created misery, hate, and war.

If God wanted to brand himself an unjust, unworthy Creator, He could have pardoned them all, could have taken them to Heaven just as He took Lincoln, Nightingale, and the others who pledged not only their devotion to Him but also their concern for the welfare of the Human Race. Against the backdrop of such people, those who

slaughtered and crippled and cheated and robbed could go to no other destiny than the fires of Hell.

As all of this rushes through my mind, the angel smiles in holy triumph — not over the damned but, rather, over those who have been saved, born again, those who didn't darken their minds and insult God. The angel speaks and a hush falls on all of us.

"It is time!" he announces. "Prepare yourselves."

We have only an instant to do so.

What sounds like a clap of thunder explodes around us, and then — without our understanding how — it happens. I had prayed about this moment for a very long time, especially those moments when life itself was so sad, so painful, so unappealing in one or more ways, and it seemed somehow balming to long for the promised joys of the perfect existence that had been conditionally promised to Mankind for thousands of years.

And now it is happening! Now the glories of eternity would be. . . .

I smile, the sweetest smile of all my years.

"Praise God," I say out loud, "praise God for. . . ."

Then the words stop, driven from me by the reality that radiated before me like a hundred million sunbeams.

Heaven.

Joy.

It sweeps over us like a sudden tidal wave yet it is quite gentle; rather than knock us down, it lifts us up. Our minds soar this time, not our spirits. All the shackles of mortality fall away. (It is difficult for me even to remember what hatred was like, to realize that once I was subject to the most unreasonable jealousy and outbursts of temper, that I polluted my body and my mind. That I did so much else. . . .)

Gone.

Drained from me like poisons from an unhealing wound. These sins have vanished. And I know that if ever the awareness of such things should re-enter, it would be merely in the light of my scorn over them, my astonishment that had permitted God's creation, my body, to be tarnished with the garbage of man's corruption.

What is Heaven like?

Mortals have asked that question for centuries. Replies have ranged from the trite to the gaudily imaginative. Not even the Bible itself is specific: an absence of sorrow, no more pain, an abundance of beauty, with streets like unto gold.

I am no longer finite. My eyes are spiritual. And I do see a place of overwhelming beauty, a beauty that delights the senses of sight, sound, and smell. I have not entered through pearly gates, contrary to legend, and there have been no trumpets but what might be called a "blast" of sensation, like that tidal wave, yes, but even more like the suddenness of a bugle at early morning, awakening those who are asleep.

None of us moves at first, so stunned are we. All any of us *can* do is stand here, impressions flooding in on us.

"It is everything I ever imagined—and yet it is so much more," someone utters.

And music!

Yes—a music of birds singing and the wind weaving through autumn trees, sighing peacefully . . . a music that combines all the joyous sounds heard on earth into one symphony with a depth and a range that makes each of us break into tears, —tears of appreciation and wonderment.

Someone asks, "How could we ever have doubted? How could we ever have risked *not* coming here?"

And I touch the person next to me and he touches someone else, and before long all of us are walking along a thoroughfare so shiny and clean, surrounded by rolling orchards and lush gardens, that we burst into song.

Beyond us is a crowd. And each one of us glimpses somebody he recognizes. I see my father who raised me and my mother who died when I was born. I don't know how—because she is standing with the others a bit of a distance away from my father—but I know it is she. I know, yes, and like a child returning home after a long absence, I run to her and we throw our arms around one another, and my father joins us.

Friends I knew who died before I did also gather around. We exchange greetings. Later we sit and talk.

"We have no hunger here, William," father remarks.

"But we do not eat?" I ask.

An Odyssey of the Soul

"There is no need. For if we had hunger, that would be a prelude to discomfort, and no source of discomfort exists here."

"But those trees over there. I thought they were apple trees, like those on our farm."

"Images from the past, son. For someone else might see pear trees and another person might not see trees, but rather, a large lake with fish so plentiful and unafraid that they jump out of the water again and again. These are only residual images, son. This is only the first stage of Heaven." My father stands and looks about him. "What I see, now, you will see soon. Though your awareness has grown already, it is not yet complete."

"Father," I ask, "what *do* you see?"

"God," he replies, smiling. "I see God."

"Mother," I ask as I stand, "you, too?"

The exaltation that is apparent on her face sends a thrill of anticipation through me.

The other "new arrivals" are getting to their feet. They are looking up. I follow their gaze.

My father rests his hand gently on my shoulder. "Son . . . ?"

I cannot speak.

Jesus is sitting in the middle of a rolling meadow. Tall stalks of golden wheatlike plants are shimmering around Him. He does not move. He seems to be smiling.

I go to Him and sit with the Master.

"How often did I pray at night, anticipating a moment such as this," I say.

"I heard you, William. I felt your love."

"You —!"

My reaction goes beyond astonishment. The Son of God *remembering!* My Savior, my Lord, remembering the humble prayer of one of seven billion human beings on Planet Earth.

"Your love helped to sustain me, good William."

No! How could even Heaven be as blessed as this? My pitiable love reaching beyond time, into eternity, and comforting the One for Whom my very soul hungered?

And I see, now, that there are no plants and we are not even in the middle of a meadow. I am seated before a throne, and on that throne is God. Beside Him is His beloved Son. I kneel as my eyes remain fixed on God, while looking also to Jesus.

"What does this mean, Master?" I ask, my voice trembling, though not with fear, but with awe, a kind of exalted realization that this is the moment toward which believers have striven through all of Man's history.

"The wheat is that through which you have passed in the old life," my Lord, my Savior, says. His voice is like honey; the kindness in His eyes overwhelms me.

"You passed through sin, through everything that is weak in the flesh, and now you have been made spirit. You are here with my Father, and Me, and we shall never be parted. We shall . . . "

As He continues speaking, an indescribable peace envelops me. I have nothing to compare with it, even the wonders of the recent past. Now I know, I know so well, what Scripture meant with the words, "The peace that passes all understanding." From the mortal part of the chronicle of our lives, we caught only glimmers. A taste. A preview. Flashes of calm, satisfaction, of. . . .

Insufficient.

All of it, unmitigated by the enslavement of fleshly desires, consumes me.

Suddenly, I turn around, and my father and my mother have appeared again.

"Wonderful, is it not?" father asks, knowing the answer.

I nod.

"The judgment?"

"Yes, good son. The judgment."

How long has it been? Possibly a day on earth but, no, it must be more than that. (A decade?) In any event, my state of mind has become more mature; I am no longer a spiritual child; I have become an adult who will never be old; I will never slow down and have to depend on pills to keep me going. All I need for refreshment is to open my eyes and absorb what is around me; nothing else is necessary.

I am next to a river which is flowing, clear as a sheet of crystal. And beside it is the Tree of Life. Christ is standing there, and as He sees me, He plucks one of the strange fruits hanging from its branches. I look at Him, and smile.

"No, Good Master, I have no need of it, nor any desire for it," I say, the words coming easily, with a happiness and a peace about them.

And we walk for a bit, my Savior and I, talking, His mind in me and mine in His and of a truth we do not speak "words" but rather exchange thoughts, bound together by the oneness promised in Scripture.

Later, I talk to people born mentally retarded who now have minds like Assisi or Luther. And the parents who deeply loved them, who stayed with them, who shared the anguish because of their tremendous faith that "all things work together for good"—have been "repaid" a thousand times, for what temporal life denied them is fully realized in Heaven. Their children now have whole minds and bodies, can converse properly, and walk without assistance.

"If Heaven offered only that," one such mother tells me, "it would be worth everything."

Those born without limbs or those who lost arms or legs or hands through accident are now restored. They have been "repaired." One woman who had never had any limbs and who remained an oddity all her life now walks about, jumping, running, and shaking hands with everyone, her face aglow.

Those once blind can see and stroll through the parks and gardens, looking with astonishment; those once deaf just sit and listen, those born mute gather in little groups and chatter away.

And me?

I had many dreams Down There. I wanted to see my parents again; I have. I wanted to walk without pain, breathe without racking coughs; and I do both now. I wanted knowledge, the answers to puzzles unsolved, questions beyond human wisdom even to formulate properly; and now I have seen back to the beginning of all things; I have watched the earth being formed, even the creation of the universe. And, most important of all, I have comprehended, without fleshly doubt of any kind, the immutable truth of everything that God ever revealed to man in centuries gone by. Ripped away are the vestiges of sin; no more seeing through a glass, darkly; no more skepticism . . . nothing that detracts from Heaven's joy.

Now I am sitting beside a golden sea. The waters are pure and clear; birds swoop overhead. No longer is it necessary for them to kill to survive. One of them lands next to me, and walks up to me. I run my hand down its back; it chatters contentedly and then takes off again. (Does it have a name? If all of God's creatures are numbered by Him, could it be that they are named by Him as well?)

Earlier, I watched as lions played with lambs. (A lamb hid behind a tree and as a lion was walking past, jumped out at it. The king of beasts yelped in

mock surprise and was about to pretend to run when it discovered the identity of the culprit. No roar escaped its jaws; instead it licked the lamb on the forehead, and the two walked off together, the lion wagging its tail, the lamb trying to wag what little he had for a tail.)

And soon I know there will be another scene, another moment of pleasure. Always, in the midst of it all, I see God. In a Heaven where descriptions based on finite calculations scarcely scratch the surface, it is impossible to say what God is like. He is not an old man with a long beard, for if His creations do not now age, how could He be expected to do so? But then God is also much more than a mere beam of light, a clap of thunder, a puffy cloud, a shimmering incandescence.

Everything around me reminds me of God. All the beauty that I see, whether by these golden waters, or the once vicious animal adversaries now playing peacefully with one another or, simply, the lack of any form of death, the eternality of existence of Heaven—this is the kingdom of God, as He always promised.

The reality of this kingdom and, hence His reality, can be understood in the satisfaction of experiencing everything we have ever wanted that wasn't contrary to divine law. The ability to soar through

the sky was a prelude to Heaven for me; with someone else it might be swimming beneath the ocean or
climbing a great mountain—experiences as diverse
as are the personalities of human beings. But even
with these illustrations, the full extent of Heaven
(and God) is merely suggested—no hunger, no
pain, no tears except of joy. Yes, but more; because
it goes beyond all such and encompasses matters
more profound: the freedom from doing *harm*, the
absence of any necessity to rely on drugs to while
away the hours. And the unique freedom which
allows total individual expression of self without the
slightest cause for divine retribution.

Behind these freedoms is yet another, that thread
which makes possible all the others, that master
pattern from which Heaven is embroidered: freedom from doubt. We no longer doubt God, for we
are *experiencing* Him and will continue to do so
throughout eternity.

What more can I say, Sarah?

As these thoughts germinate, so does my eager-
ness for the day when you will arrive here. Perhaps,
before such time, your spirit also will soar about the
world. Did we not share a similar desire? It may be
that you, too, visit places you've wanted to visit for
so long. The lines of age will be gone, and you will

be young again; your steps will be strong and vibrant, your. . . .

I can look down at you now, Sarah. I can see everything you are doing. At this moment you and the children and their children are sitting before the fireplace, watching flames dance over the logs. It is winter Down There and the warmth of the fire feels good to you. You are saying that it seems as though I am still there, that you can sense me hovering nearby.

You get up and go into my den, pausing a moment to look at my desk, and some photographs framed and hung on the wall. Tears start but you stop them quickly. You bow your head, your lips moving in prayer.

A voice breaks into my thoughts. I look up. Approaching me along the golden shore is a tall, handsome young man. His body is strong, healthy, well-muscled, and he moves with athletic grace.

"Father, will mother be joining us soon?"

I smile.

"Yes, John . . . quite soon.

And we walk together through paradise.

My name is Sarah.

I just died.

Sarah!

William! I —
must tell you
what has happened.

I think I know, my darling.

You do?

Yes . . .
it's something
to
do
with
soaring!